LADDERS OF LOVE

ZEENAT FATIMA

FanatiXx Publication

AM/56, Basanti Colony, Rourkela 769012, Odisha
ISO 9001:2015 CERTIFIED
Website: *www.fanatixx.in*

" *LADDERS OF LOVE*"

By: ZEENAT FATIMA

ISBN: 978-93-89557-57-2

English & Hindi Poetry & Stories

1st Edition

BOOK FORMATTING: MAYURI VALANJU
BOOK COVER: SAGAR SAMAL
PRESENTED BY: REASONS AND LAUGHTER

DISCLAIMER

This is a work of fiction. Our editors have tried their best to edit the content of all the author/authors and check the plagiarism. All the write-ups in this book are unique and are only published in this book.

In case any plagiarism or error is found, the author is the sole responsible and not the publisher.

ACKNOWLEDGMENT

I thank Almighty for every reason of my life.

I would like to thank my family and friends who have always supported me in every phase of my life.

I would like to thank **Japneet Kaur** the founder of *Reason and Laughter* for providing me this golden opportunity to work for **LADDER OF LOVE**, and providing this beautiful platform for amateurs. I would like to thank FanatiXx publication for publishing us.

Last but not the least I would like to thank all the co-authors of this anthology for making it a success. Being patient and having faith in us, co-operating, supporting and encouraging me in every step while making this anthology.

This anthology is based on multiple emotions of the budding artists which are depicted in the form of short stories, poems, articles, micro tales in Hindi and English.

COMPILER

ZEENAT FATIMA

"Zeenat Fatima is a 21-year-old girl, a resident of Ranchi. Pursuing English Hons. She is a simple girl leading her life in a very simple way. She writes to express herself. She writes poems and short tales and is a nature lover too. She expresses herself through her words with the creativity of the words and then loves giving it a voice and presenting it to people. She is into speeches as well and has a little dream to be a TED speaker. She has an interest in reading books too as she believes that they are the best companions, she reads thoroughly and extensively to write in a better way and enhances the same.

Instagram handle : _never_ending_feelings_

FOUNDER

JAPNEET KAUR

Japneet Kaur, daughter of Mr. Surjeet Singh and Mrs. Dilpreet Kaur was brought up in Indirapuram, UP. She is pursuing German language and BA programming course from Delhi University. She is a passionate writer who loves to pen down her emotions and environment and strive to make her parents proud. She is even working on her very first novel making her one step closer to her goal.

Instgram : @sheedreamss

EDITOR

MAYURI VALANJU

Mayuri Valanju, resident of Mumbai. She is a commerce graduate pursuing higher education. Social Media Head of Fanatixx and Fanatixx Publications. Co-author of many anthologies. Her debut book is 'Spectrum of Thoughts'. Writing is Peace for her. She is addict of Korean, Turkish and Chinese dramas. Coffee is her love and sound of book pages flipping like her the most. Connecting with people and talking to them is what she loves.

You can find her on instagram @scribblers_abode.

DESIGNER

SAGAR SAMAL

Sagar Samal is a Photographer, Image Manipulation and Colour Grading Artist.
Hardworking with a "Create Something Awesome" Mentality.
A graduate in Bachelor of Computer Application but an Artist By Heart.

Instagram : photosign.cf

NICKUNJ JOSHI

8

There is a storm running inside my heart. Which can only be calmed by her hug.

***

Sometimes apologies can't heal the damage, which was done by actions.

***

SIMRAN NISHCHAL

You will never know how many nights I've spent while trying to figure out what you find so special in her ignorance than my attention.

***

UTKANTH VASOYA

Find Someone Who Wants to Invest in You, See You Win ,
Support Your Vision , And Fall in Love With You Daily.
Someone Who Motivates you to Become a Better person
And Shows you the potential you Dont See in Your Self.

***

the Real POWER of a man is in the size of the smile of the
Woman (life partner) sitting next to him..

***

SHAHREEN KAHKASHA

11

Love is like a bulb, which when glows brightens your life

And when fuses,darkens the life.

***

POEMS

JAPNEET KAUR

Let's go on a walk at night,
Near the ocean let's feel alive,
Be my charm who would make me laugh,
Let's lay under the sheet of thousands stars,
Let me look at the magic,
Shadow of stars which falls on the ocean isn't tragic,
Hold my hand firmly,
And let me adore the beauty of the moon,
Look at me as if I m the best thing that has ever happened to you,
Maybe you don't have to wait any longer,
Let me say 'look! The moon is soo beautiful. The beauty is attracting me towards itself'
And then,
Just look into my eyes by holding my hand say 'I can see my moon sitting next to me'
Let me blush and again adore the beauty of the moon and then,
Tell me 'The moon has flaws but my moon is flawlessly beautiful'
Make me smile like never before,
Let me be yours and you be mine,
Leave rest of the things for life.

AKSHAT DIXIT

HER HEART WAS WHISKEY EMBERS

Her soul was like whiskey.

Not to be tasted all at once.

But to be sipped.

With the passing hours.

Of every cold winter night

And her heart was fire, Wild.

She asked me if i wanted to catch it.

But her eyes spoke the truth.

She was free.

And so i ran with it.

***

SUMMER OF ISOLATION

And As The Sand Of Time Escaped Our Toes.
. We Left Our Footprints On It.
Running Towards Sunsets
Drinking Champagne Out Of Bottles.
Skinny Dipping On The Beaches.
Writing Our Names Under The Stars.
Laughing On Stories Untold.
And Amidst All Of That Chaos.
I Found Myself, While Looking Into Your Eyes.
And Fell In Love. With The Idea Of Arriving At My Death,
Warm. And In Love. With You.

DHRUV DARJI

DEMON INSIDE

Will you love the demon inside me?
I know there is a darkness in my soul that sinks down into
the abyss, and my heart beats callously.
I cannot pretend to be an angel,
I don't aspire for Sainthood,
I never have presumed that I was good,
and never sought to be better than this.
Will you tremble at the sight of me?
Revile within the truth of me, do I repulse you so?
Or might you glimpse something beyond all the insanity,
can you see past the nightmares of my dreams?
Understand I am not seeking to be saved,
I don't want to be led astray from my twisted path.
Don't come to me if you believe you can purify my soul,
but I want your willingness to dare to enter the labyrinth
with me. We could learn to destroy each other beautifully,
we will not live in petty lies, and falsetto hopes.
Our lives may derail in time, but they will be entirely ours,
the wreckage of truth which refuses to be denied.
Do you have enough faith in yourself to risk all your safety
ground, for the perilous position of my love ?

MOHAMMED UMAR M

HAPPINESS

We nowadays tend to make our lives,
Always sadder and blame others.
For not being happy or being sad.
Actually it's our fault,
We can find, Happiness in every single thing we do.
It's the way we look at it, and think.
We can be happy even if it's negative,
Just think why it has been happened
May be there is something happy to it
If we find ways to be happy in every way
Then no one can stop us from being happy.

PRABEER DEEPAK

Love- A temporary Attachment

Yes, it was a feeling of intense affection, people named it as
love.

It all started with emotions with a hither and thither phase
Moments fluctuated at a pace
Heartbeats begun the race
You entered in a way And made my mind sway.
Imaginations became real
Life turned as a deal
Your smile became the key
To the locks Hidden in my heart sea.
You easily stole my thought
Where my heart got caught Love was just a name
To see you happy ,became my aim.
You reserved a seat in my heart
Making every of me as your part
Respect was just an art
You played pretty smart.

S K NANDINI

LOVE IS TO FEEL

Love is a beautiful feeling, which We can only feel !
I don't know how to love,
but You're the one who made me to feel the love,
You cared me,
I melt in your forehead kisses,
Breath my air and feel my love
After feeling every inch of your love
Suddenly you left me apart,
I feel like crying aloud, but I don't want to cry,
because You have cheated me,
Why should i want to cry for you,
You where my everything,
I never expected some day i will loose you,
I can't imagine anyone in your place
I am really very glad to have you Again in my life,
Around millions of people I can feel you ,
I want you in my life I couldn't still believe that You're moved
on from me,

Everyday when I wake up, I check my inbox to see your
messages but I don't get upset because my love is true ,
One day you'll accept me as your life .....
I am all yours and you're mine.

PRADEEPTI SHARMA

THE COLOR OF LOVE

A life went by, another is still waiting
What I left behind, and what I am still contemplating,
Moments of connubial bliss can never be bargained with
anything, A longing for togetherness is all I am deeply
wanting.

The revelry of the heart is by your close presence,
No festivities seem complete in your absence.
The color of your love and care is this soul's true essence,
All other colors seem a fleeting part of this existence.
Today, I desire to color myself orange and red,
To preserve the sanctity of the unbreakable thread.
And, then I sprinkle a little blue,
To revisit your caresses, bearing softness like the morning
dew.

And, then I pour hues of green,
To feel the depth of your touch, so balmy, and serene.
Finally, I splatter lime and yellow,
To dance to the tunes of your husky voice, so soothing,
and mellow.
So, I played Holi, and I danced, I rejoiced, I laughed,
And, I did it all in your love.
You are far away to fulfill life's existential needs,

SHILPA KRISHNA

REMEMBER TO SURVIVE

There are times,
Where feelings overflow
and You are unable to see through it
You drown and frown in those emotions,
Praying for a raft to save you from it.
But then you need to remember,
You survived deeper storms before
Which almost sunk your sailing ship
And still you made your way to the shore.
So, let it all break lose and
Be the strength that you found
Be the choice that you made,

You are what survival is made up of.

SUMEGHA S

LOVE AFFECT

You In Me
He sensed my eye
It tears with joy,
He sensed my ear
It demands for same sound,
He kissed my lips
It's craving to receive unlimited,
He affected my heart
By his affection,
He made by nerves get hold of him
He touched my inner Universe
Spreading the sparkle of Love.

BURHANUDDIN SHAYAR

SOMEONE'S MEMORIES

Those early morning walks
Every day and night we used to talk
Missing those days those walks and talks
You are my heartbeat and ticking clock.
You are the only clock ticking in my heart
You are far away from me
but also my heart dart
You are not missing
i feel your presence my sweet heart
Your memories your thought are always in my heart
No matter how far you are
You are in my mind and in my heart
My heart beat beats with your memories.

DIMPLE GEHANI

BLEEDING EMOTIONS

Let my emotions bleed
Let my heart bleed
It was dark every where.
. When we had something to share..
Now let my happiness bleed
It isn't me because I laugh every time..
Oh yes i remember my soul cries some time....
Let my soul bleed.
Why I am the way i am
Today let my ego bleed
Tell me if I was wrong
Tell me if I asked something so strong
Tell me now where I belong
Or let my trust bleed
If no than why you took my lead,
Lets promise we wont ever meet.
Lets promise we will be strangers without need
Right I remember that date was just a small treat..
Ohk let my memories bleed...
I am moving on now...
My laughter is real not vague
Let me tell you I am now happy not rage
Because I have learned from that cage
I am finding myself eagerly
Let my old things bleed
Let my old soul bleed.....

SWATI MISHRA

My Favorite Mistake

Your first cry made me screech
Your midnight crises won't let me breath
Love we made, I remember he said
Was she really?
Or is she a mistake?
I hold her now with him all gone.
Her selfless eyes brew inside my heart
Her hysterical giggles, my reason to laugh.
Her subtle rise and fall,
Oh I love, the way she walks.
A mistake, is what now they call.
Can't deny you were my fault
But nothing would I take, glitters or stake.
My lovely favorite mistake,
for you I give'em all.

SAERA S

DIVINAL THOUGHT

When ever I grow,
Deeper in my thought,
I always ask the universe,
What might you be doing,
Are you also thinking about me,
Standing in your terrace,
Listening to the chirping of birds,
Watching sky change it's shades,
From blue to pinkish blue,
Fading away into black,
Or maybe taking out a little time,
From your busy schedule,
Just for yourself,
Sharing secrets with your soul,
And maybe adding in some more about me.
What might you be doing,
Listening to soothing music or rock,
Thinking about us and our world,
Or trying to take a short escape by dreaming,
And then hiding it even from yourself,
Maybe you wants to share,
Maybe you wants to be understood,
Or maybe just wants to stay,
in this moment, Connecting yourself with the universe.

What might you be doing,
Releasing this question to the higher being,
I stand still, With sparking eyes,
To hear the reply,
But the universe in returns says,
Wait my child, For Good things takes time,
All your questions will be answered,
What you have asked for, is DIVINE.
He will come to you, And stay with you,
I wouldn't say forever
But till the soul lives,
You too will be affixed,
With love overflowing,
And peace by your side,
Our hands will always be on both of you,
Just be receptive,
Freeing this question in their hands,
I set back and relax,
Until the next time,
I have a question, for you again in my mind.

SHAHREEN KAHKASHA

LOVE JOURNEY

When two hearts meet,
Differences washed under feet,
And love is at its peak.
Do this lasts forever?
No inkling of what will stay ever.
But, Still seems veracity in every vows,
because love pervades your soul with aroma of rose.
Every seconds I'm hothead to meet you,
and every bit of my eyes wants pretty you,
YEAH, Love fastens you so tightly,
that even your bad flash starts shine brightly,
It seems bringing happiness in every bit of ocean drop.
Hello! Darling Now, you are my prop.
Sharing future is all we dream.
Proposing each other is all we scream.
Yeah, you and I will together forever.
This time love will create a history,
which will itself became a mystery.

ASHISH VASUDEVA

THE MOON BABY

The truth was so stinging that he couldn't withhold,
Just like the night itself,
Cold and bold.
Silent beyond silence,
It wouldn't let him cope.
But he was a moon baby,
He found his hope.

Cause he himself is the night that covers the sky.
He himself is the eye that is all left dry.
He believes there is a remedy for all of our scars.
For it is the night only,
That brings out the stars...

DHIRAJ ARORA

DESIRES

I desire to call you mine
, with every morning, new sunshine.
To be with you my whole life,
I desire you to be my side.
I desire to come in your dreams,
to calm you, whenever you scream.
The sadness and pain of your way,
I desire to take it all away.
All night I desire, to look at your eyes,
when I feel scared,
will have a sleep on your thighs.
To be with you in every shadow and heat,
I desire to be with you like your heartbeat.
I desire to be someone u desire,
I will be water you will be my fire.
To tell you my poems firstly ever,

I desire us to be together like this forever!

ARUN PATIL

HER

Like a rainbow at the corner of storm ,
She entered his life,
Colour amidst the grey ,
Peace amidst the chaos.

Just like the moon brings high tide .
She brought happiness to his life ,
Nothing brightened up the day better than her.

Just like a philosopher with his thoughts ,
He thought of her all day .
Her smile her eyes and oh her hair,

He would give up anything to be with her,
For with her he felt the way he always needed.
The comfort had no comparison.

For it was her who had made him lose,
his appetite as well as his sleep.
The fear of losing her kept him awake,
While the happiness of having her fed his appetite.

PRIYA V. VASWANI

LOVE ME BACK

If I tell you
I need you
I genuinely mean that I need you
If I say I need you
I probably trust you
To catch me
When I am falling

I can be Sunny on some days
I can be Gloomy on others
I can be Hell on some days
I can be Heaven on others
You have to experience both
To understand the Awkward Beauty in Me

I would love to get compliments
Compliments about my
Purity of Soul
And Beautiful thoughts

I can find out the Luxury
Just at doing Nothing
Staring at Heaven
Staring at Stars
and Admiring them

If I am rough to you
If I am breaking you
It is probably
When I am trying to Mend you

In this era
of fakeness
I can be the permanent reason
To the genuine smile of yours
If I care about you ,
I can take enormous of efforts,
To keep your happiness alive.
Little I expect ,
The affectionate gesture back.

Let me be ,
The way I am.
Accept me,
The way I am.
Love me back,
The way I am.

SHRUTI SINGH

Unspoken Words Of Summernight

She was embracing the moon in summer night
Running naked to the beach under moonlight
And when she smiled
All the stars came alive
In thunderclaps,
he sat beside
Popped the bottles of champagne
And looked at her as if heavens knew her name.

***

WILD POET

With a only broken heart left
She decided to grow, she did.
Fragile of that she is pretending
But She was a wildgirl
She decided to put her tears in poetries over crying at nights
She chooses to become a Wildpoet.

RIYA DAS

Falling love

Are falling stars the tears of angels
shed when two lovers don't confess?
how unfortunate it is,
that with falling stars the sky is so overly dressed.
They spend their lives in grief
and with ache their hearts are laid
and they wait and they wait
for their love to fade.
When they could have gotten all that their hearts wished,
yes, they could have stood underneath
a red velvet sky and kissed.
But nothing can bring back the moments gone by -
Look, another star breaks high up in the sky.

GOPI MANOJ

AN UNTOLD LOVE STORY

I love you not for your beauty
But for the beauty of your soul.
I love you not for your richness
But for the richness of your heart .
I love you not for your beautiful smile
But for making people around to smile.
I love you not for your success
But for the struggle, you had for it.
I love you not for your stories you tell
But for motivating them with those stories .
I have many reasons to love you
But, you still ignore me and hate me.
People around me think that I was mad,
But, poor fellows don't know to find a gem stone is easy,
but Kohinoor like you is rare.
I love you forever and ever till last breathe.

SHIVAM

Beautiful morning

I wake up one beautiful morning,
and the sun was shining like it does,
then suddenly a breeze whispered in my ears are you happy?
I said "maybe not.
maybe the reason was you weren't there,
but wait a minute why i was pretending that i don't care...
then suddenly the same breeze turned those ugly pages,
and very next moment
I just wanted to be Happy
even after knowing that this happiness
won't last for ages...

GOURAV CHAPLOT

Life

Dreams are the choice to alive
when I'm deeply alone realise
try to find happiness around
but got hurted by all-around
try to figure out the things
but got stuck with the pain
possibilities are less to live
but my faith is still alive...

SANI HOSSAIN

Assured loan of liability

I beg a debt of share !
Share of endless love and care !!
With the tiny sap of Trust you can ever rely !
Surely, I won't have any act towards it to deny !!
Selflessly, I swear the worthy end to bring forth !
I will invest the every concern & need for proving my worth !!
From mending the delicate wounds and the unfitted crumbs !
Would toil the labour to the toughest lumps !!
Upon the mighty Crown I leave the every conditions to be
favoured!

No matter what may,
or it's the hurdled turbulence from
Which it needed to be savoured !!
Bravo! The promised labour soon gonna meet and pay for sure
As the debt of share begged ardently,
with all those unsoothing pains he's to endure!!

Assertion of love

Love is never about the wild kisses to moist the thirst;
The tight hug of Bossoms fulfilling the untamed lust !!
Striping the body to taste the flesh, more mad
actions of intimacy, with the Love reality so less.!!
Hangouts in the uncared, untouched place,
uncared about the insecured solace.!!
Celebration of a customary (Valentine)day,
but an obligation, vow for each &every day.!!
Love is all about the embrace & wait,
Untill the one desired & worthy is met.!!
Towards each other with all due Respect,
Having the absolute care,
faith and every compromising concern,
keeping all the odd cravings & desires in dern.!!
Enjoying the licit pleasures with the concern
and inhibition of Divine punishment,
dealing with perfection to harvest a pure
and sound Relation ever
without any further unforeseen
and illicit commitment.!!

FREYA SHAH

OUR STORY

I don't know how to jot down our story on the soft corners of
heart.

Maybe it will be harsh
or maybe it is going to heal all the wounds..
Maybe it will be deep inscribed
or maybe with the flow of blood,
the story even gets rubbed off..
Maybe we share a heart to heart connection
and you get pricked
and come out of the bad dream
and maybe we are back together...

<u>CLUTCHED SOUL</u>

I had always dreamt of us together
but maybe something pinched me hard
and my dream broke.
When your lips touched my forehead
I would taste our future together..
When our hands clutched our souls even got attached..
The bond which we shared was even stronger than the
diamond..

When my eyes see you they still glow even more brighter
than the sun.

They say time heals everything..
But that is what we are running out off....

***

SOMMAIYA

The Pain In The Rhyme

Why can't we be the sea
Calm composed Singing like Glee
Why can't we see
The pain in rhyme
And the explicit enemy
Why can't we be me
The fine charm
And the aura key
Why couldn't we flee
Like the birds chirping
Suffering-free
Why couldn't we cry
The last guy
Was atleast meant to try
Why couldn't we judge
The forehead lines
The stick-face budge
Why couldn't we just speak
The truth that was needed
Rather lie was the thing that was greeted
Our words got masked
The mind was subconscious
The lips were inflated
The reality never came out.

NOORASH PARVEEN

DRENCHED

Two faces, smiling under the grime
A photograph in drawer and something lost in time
Sipping my tea,
I write this poem
Which like our tale is gonna lose its rhyme

Maybe drunk on the rain,
I'll spill the secret
Locked by you, sealed by time in my heart's casket
I thought that the night was gonna suck me forever
But no, I see light, I'm light,
maybe you were my mascot

But this drizzle asks,
could the tale have been continued?
And if yes, this time,
would my feelings be valued?

Sipping my tea,
I wonder, in your place too does it rain so much?
And sitting against the window do you ever long for my touch?
But then again,
you never like the rain

My tea cup is empty now,
maybe it's just emptiness in my clutch

Except for this rainy days,
I've forgotten all the was and were
Except for this rainy days, nothing makes me sip slower!!

***

POOJA RAVAL

FRAGRANCE

It was an awesome opportunity to be pure
While the earth had love and then petrichor

Its too difficult to have a smile though
I console my self that I am fine

Not always but frequently
I was in search atleast for supine

It was never my arrogance or attitude
However i try sometime for solitude

For those small happiness and small achievements
I love to be idyllic and express my enjoyment
I am the person who is pluviophile
Clinomania always bring a big smile
This can not be efflorescence of the thoughts
It's actually the fragrance what realme can brought

***

<u>Euphoria</u>

It's my dream to love you the most
Without any hesitation or fear of lost
It's always the best thing of my life
To be with you and having honour of your wife
It's only the love who had hold us
The embience of amour only can catch us
It's love to roam around the world
With you and your three magical word.

***

SARAANSH AGARWAL

TEENAGER FEELINGS

Feelings
What are they?
To them, To these pitiful strangers, madly in love.
Running into each other every day,
Every day, ignoring what they truly felt.
Love that blossomed like a hyacinth
on a beautiful spring morning,
Or like the birth of a flower sprouting out of the bud.
One of them needed to act up, or to their regret,
Their love will slowly manage to
dissipate into the empty nothingness of heartbreak.
He loved her, And, ohh, She loved him, too.
They dreamed of each other;
How they would be.
How they could laugh together,
and smile together, and share, their gentle goodnights.
But, For now, They remain apart,
Ignoring their burning thoughts and too strong feelings.
Slowly falling into their own demise.
A demise without love.
A demise without each other.

SANJANA

A Guardian Angel.

I asked my guardian angel, Is it where it ought to be ?
Right behind me, above my shadow,
Didn't somebody send it to me ?
Angel, angel ! You're so beautiful !
Did my God send you down ?
My God is my love and rules my world
I'm sure He'll never let me down !
My angel smiled, came down to it's knees.
It's nectarine eyes were meant to please.
It held my hands, looked right in the eyes,
What it said next, didn't feel really nice.
"The man whose heart you broke sent me here.
Your sadness, misfortune and tears were his fear.
I ain't your guardian angel,
you don't deserve one.
All I wanna do to you is shun."
"Your words broke him into bits and pieces.
Your actions reduced him to the darkest of ashes.
You did him wrong,
turned his world upside down.
He gathered himself,
from every scattered piece he found."
"You deserve penance for losing your sanctity.
You will weep one day for showing your vanity.
If I weren't his angel,
I would set you on fire.

With twigs, logs and you,
in the flames of a pyre."
Saying so, the angel slipped away.
Disappearing into the moonlight
, never to come back any day.
I stood there staring at the dark empty sky,
Screaming at myself,
"Why did I do this ? Why ?"
I felt vulnerable, as brittle as glass.
Helpless and defenceless,
with every moment that passed.
This was the beginning,
of a hideous phase,
That would probably last, for the rest of all my days.
I'd spend sleepless nights,
waiting for the angel to alight.
Falling to my knees,
repenting for my sins,
maybe I'd stop losing my mind.
I waited and waited,
but it never returned.
My life's now diminished to emptiness,
losing everything I ever earned.

ARTICLES

TARUN JEEVNANI

It's been seen that from the time of our birth till the time of our
death we live in a state of motion and in this state we
experience a lot of things, the good and the bad ,
we all have our share of experience.
Now, we have a little something we call emotions, as we are
humans these emotions come naturally to us
we have an emotion for every action/talk/occasion,
but the emotion we all have in common from time to time is
love.

 Yes love as much as it can make our silliest dreams come true
it does not happen over , it has to be build between two
persons.

 It has numerous ways on how it can be build but not everyone
understands that when a good bond is build it has to be build
using hardwork/compassion/selflessness/ and pretty much
every selfish thoughts you have coz being in love means you
have to be able to take a stand for your love.
All these little efforts combine together to form of a ladder and
this ladder of love is so vulnarable that even the slighest mis-
judgement can cause it to break, so always believe in your love
and have a high determination for it coz it can take you places
and can even let you see the stars you only dreamed of.

ANEEK SULTAN

THE SIXTH AMENDMENT

A dream amended So it took me a heavy dose of homesickness complimented with the surge of nostalgia to realize that ever since I had the slightest insight of politics and the political space in Kashmir, the term ⍰Sadr-e-Riyasat⍰ had been striking a chord in me. The people in Kashmir are rather more apt to show interest in politics, more specifically in the concept of abnegating it.Given the horrors that the conflict unfolded, people do want at some point in time to feel in control of the happenings.Or maybe just the absence of being in a never-ending stance of constraint.But what held this term so dear me? What made me sao interested? Was it just the sound of it, or maybe the authority therein?

Maybe the answer lied in the deprivation.The mere absence of an entity makes people crave for it more! And this deprivation has been known to unfurl the most powerful of insurrections.Who knows deprivation like the Kashmiris do! The bloodcurdling conflict has an uncanny ability to toy with people, their actions, their prejudices and even at times rare, dreams.And this goes beyond story-telling.The frantic attempts to rescue an entire population have been mostly cosmetic, not to mention the extent they pushed people further to at times.The people have endured misconduct at all levels possible- physical, psychological and emotional.So much so that people have stopped whining about it Getting back to what Kashmiris glorify and at times curse-the history behind the post of Sadr-e-Riyasat.   Till 30 Mar 1965, Kashmir had its two prominent posts- Wazir-e-Azam (Prime Minister) and the other being Sadr-e-Riyasat (President) which were later replaced with Chief Minister and Governor respectively.It was this ill-starred day that the autonomy that people had been cherishing withered away and the mass sentiment was set at naught. So how did this demotion of titles come about? It was after ⍰The Constitution of Jammu & Kashmir (Sixth Amendment) Act 1965 amended the State Constitution and replaced ⍰Sadri Reyasat⍰ by Governor. Prior to this, Meher Chand Mahajan, Sheikh Muhammad Abdullah, Bakshi Ghulam Muhammad, Khwaja Shamsuddin and Ghulam Muhammad Sadiq had served as Wazir-e-Azam of the State while Karan Singh was Sadr-e- Riyasat.But once the amendment was made in 1965, Ghulam Muhammad Sadiq and Karan Singh became the first Chief Minister and Governor of the State respectively. However, what is more intriguing is the fact that the amendment not only changed the nomenclature but also the founding premise on which the post of Sadr-e-Riyasat is based. The post of Sadr-e-Riyasat, an elective, as is provided in Section 27 of the constitution, was to be elected by people of the State through their representatives in State Legislatures.The amendment provided that the post, now called the governor, is to be appointed by the President, unlike earlier times. This was a historical amendment as it did away with the constitutional autonomy of the state .The move was quoted 'unconstitutional by the High court of Jammu and Kashmir', given that the amendment meant to change the basic structure of the constitution.The court observed, ⍰The elective status of head of the state (Sadr-e-riyasat) was an important attribute of constitutional autonomy enjoyed by the state, a part of the ⬚basic framework⬚ of the state constitution and – therefore – not within the amending power of the state legislature⬚. The court, however, left it to the legislatures to turn things around.Did the state legislature take it forward? Apart from belligerent debates, a foot- stomping no is the answer! Yet again, Kashmiris took a shellacking, not knowing the future consequences thereof. The amendment, though seemingly a slight change of names, hit the state autonomy quite hard as now the two posts were commensurate with other states.This undermined the special status that the state of Jammu and Kashmir had been endowed with. The conflict made it almost impossible for some posts to be pursued.This, most visibly, left a vacuum only to grow stronger with the sixth amendment adding to the desperation. There were a few passionate attempts to turn the wheel back, yet in vain as the dispensation could never make the move again.People in Kashmir have realized over time where the real might lies. So who do blame for snatching the dream, a dream to serve my land? Could it be the people for instance, or should I point fingers at the dispensation who outrightly rejected the bill to revive the prestigious title of Sadr-e- Riyasat? Or should I put the blame on myself for dreaming of something so improbable? With the sixth amendment, was amended a dream that I was yet to dream of -Becoming the Sadr-e-Riyasat of Kashmir someday!

SHORT STORIES

ZEENAT FATIMA

TAKEN AT DUSK

It was chilling December, everybody was excited for Christmas and new year, two people were about to bake their love story.

This is a love story of two young people who lived in two different cities, but were best friends. The boy loved the girl and had proposed her, but she was not ready for the relationship. But their bond remained same.

Like every day, they were sharing about the things happened on that day. Suddenly, she confessed her feelings for him. He got surprised as he thought she was not ready for the commitment.

She doesn't love him, but couldn't see her best friend sad. She knew her best friend was broken, and was alone. She decided to give it a shot. And who knew, she would fall in love soon.

Every morning, she used to wake him up through phone call, and used to fall in love with his sleepy voice. She desperately waits for the clock to strike 12, just to talk to him. Though it was a long distance relationship they never felt the distance. By every passing day, their love started growing deeper. She was an introvert, he was a friendly charm. Together they were creating their story - A beautiful love story. He decided to make her wishes come true, she decided to keep him happy.

It was the 6th month, she was on cloud nine. She like a small kid wished to celebrate their 6 months of togetherness. "Baby it's 7th of may!" She texted him.

He was online but never replied. She waited for him to reply but he never did. She even tried to call few a times but he didn't respond.

He called her at that evening, she got upset so she never answered to his call.

He texted her "sorry Kishmish, I got stuck with some work"

"Just one call, you could have answered. I was so happy about our 6 months of togetherness, but you have devastated the zeal." She replied furiously.

"Baby, was really busy, I got tired and slept, from next time I will not repeat my mistake" he tries to convince her.

"It's ok" she replied.

"Guess whom I am talking to!" he asked.

"How would I know whom you are talking! " she replied still in a bad mood.

"I had told you about my best friend few days back, she is in the town and wants to meet me. I am super excited to see her!!!" he feverishly texted.

" yeah right, go meet her, talk to her .why are you even talking to me? Take care , enjoy her company. Bye! "She blew out on him and logged off.

The intimacy of the situation was understood by him, he knew his kishmish was upset. He posted her picture on Instagram saying "Love, I feel blessed to have you in my life. I always make mistakes and hurt you, but you always let off things, and have accepted my imperfection whole heartedly. Finally, completed 6th month of togetherness and counting more. Baby, I want to hold your hand forever and together want to grow old."

The very next morning when she opened her Instagram she saw that post and was astonished, her heart melted. Again he won her heart. With teary eyes she called him and apologized for last nights' behavior.

They started planning for their first date, as they longed to meet desperately.

"I wanna meet you shona." She said in a child like voice.

"Want to meet you too baccha" he said.

And finally the day came. He came to meet her. They went on a date just the way she wanted. Far from city's hustle and bustle, in the laps of nature. There, he went on his knees and proposed her "Will you be mine forever?" She knodded yes and he slid the ring in her finger, and started to blush. Tears rolled out from her eyes, all her wish were coming true. He always basked her with the radiance of his love , and his love reflected on her face, in her smile and in her glittery eyes. The moment was ecstatic. Both were gratified to see each other. At that moment , they hugged each other, as if it were their last hug.

And alas! It was their last hug. While returning home, it started raining heavily ,they started enjoying that moment too, but suddenly they met with an accident. They both were heavily injured struggling and fighting to stay alive but unfortunately nature has to play its game, they died.

ANIRUDH SHREENATH

TULASI- THE BOOK OF HIS LOVE

Kaagi was a Man with a routine of formal suits, five days, ten hours desk job with various work timings placed inside a concrete atmosphere with facilities that crippled his skills by being habituated with mechanical work ethic. He saw himself as a modern age hardworking wage labour who worked under hardening mental stress rather than being physical. Especially when he found his weekends enjoyable only while partying; this reminded him of his previous generations' labours who get their weekly wages and gets drunk to be liberated from the physically burned out stress.

Kaagi being one such man, had a search for purpose that was more meaningful and charitable, finally found a small shelter with Tulasi. Tulasi was a colleague from a different department at his office, Kaagi developed a beautiful feeling towards Tulasi by admiring her, by the long wait to see her at workplace, he loved her hair, he liked the way she spoke, her tender skin tone, in all ways he was infatuated   by   her.
He wanted her to bring changes in his life, he expected moments spent with her to be memories till the end of his life, he wanted to make love with her, but all of these desires only brought an innocent smile on his face. He was never confident enough to take few steps towards her to speak out his feel, they both did not belong to same religion, He did not have an asset value of his own, he did not have an aggressive attitude to grab whatever he aspired, he did not belong to any specific urbanised communities, his attire made no grandeur, his visions were not much ambitious, his image on the practical world was   very   small.

He had one special quality that made him a standout from others. He knew a lot to admire and abundantly love and cherish the admiration towards anything that was done out of heart. He stood hesitant to convey all this and had a clear picture of being surrounded by various boundaries and multiple hurdles to reach her. Hence he surrendered the unconditional emotion to fate.

"Emotions are not man made, to feel emotions are a gift given by nature itself. A gentle breeze would definitely make a man smile, warmth gives him serenity, hot scorching Sun triggers an inter tempest." Unlike all these, whenever he stood abandoned or unrecognized of his love, he moved away from people. Yet a couple of sparrows and butterflies came near him in search of something. Initially he felt unfamiliar but later realised that to one such tendered heart; there were lots of wonderful creatures and people in search of abundant love to be received and cherished.

Kaagi went in search of love to receive and cherish in abundance; as he had so much to share; he started to find them in unimaginable places. He discovered love in the sideways of the roads with homeless people, he felt love recognized and treated specially with great acceptance in the slums, he felt love cheerfully accepted inside the shelters of the hill top estate labours, he recognized orphan children loved him to the core when quality time and hugs were spent with them rather than only donating food and clothing. He found a lot more and finally decided to write about them.

He continued his journey and made his heart bigger and wider by breaking down all boundaries to love and be loved, a lot. He shared few of his experiences in his first book after he understood the fact that "love is beyond marriage, sensuality and carrying a relationship. If a heart could give so much love, it should definitely be given to the person without any hesitation, be it accepted or rejected."   The book started with a preface like this: "Tulasi, has always been a medicinal & religious plant that was treated to serve to the Gods by cleansing with pure water. It was used for all medical purposes. The Tulasi Thara- a stand made out of concrete, filled with mud at the centre head portion, where the saplings were planted. The thara had a religious symbol outlined that determines a border in the name of auspicious treatment. This being the image given to a naturally grown plant had so much categorization and margins created by humans but were not naturally forced to be accepted by all consciousness. I wondered why was only rose romanticized and not Tulasi? Leaf petals of Tulasi kept in between the flock of hair with its fresh wetness, any woman would carry beauty at its epitome but with much prejudiced concrete structures defined, none would seem to approach even if romance and love was felt towards the plant instead of respect. No matter how much we draw signs or propagate ideals, the emotion comes without any notion because that is natural and pure by itself. Human emotions and nature shares a strong common bond, hence in one way or the other it reaches its ends unconditionally."

A Kid's view about education...

On a sudden evening, a kid was so disturbed about things that he learned about life. It never struck him until once he heard a new term that people used regularly. The moment he heard that term for the first time, it took few minutes to receive it and later he was never convinced about a partial explanation about the same, and he went to his mother and asked his doubt.

The kid asked, "Mom, you taught me that we all had only one life but people are talking about two different lives?" Initially, the mother couldn't understand the context of the question, she then asked what made him ask this question and he started to narrate the conversation which he had with his school friend earlier the same day. Kid: Mom I was having a conversation with my friend about education, I asked her if education was sharing knowledge to one another, why was the concept of school fees? For that, she said, "without paying fees the teachers wouldn't get money to eat." I found it a bit convincing but it again bothered me and I asked "Why were the books charged?" She said, "This money is for the people who printed it." Yet it didn't convince me then I asked her, "Why do we want to buy a book when we can lend it from the library for free?"

She again had an answer where she said, "Not all can get books at the same time, the library does not have sufficient books." Yet I wasn't able to get myself satisfied and it made me ask my question, "alright if knowledge is sharing as teachers always said, why are ranks and marks?" She quickly said, "Without ranks and marks how would you know who's the best and the worst?" I asked her "is education a running race?" And she answered, "it is a healthy competition." I was not done, hence I asked, "Okay but if that's the case why were failed students detained on the same class for another year?" She couldn't stand any longer, she got annoyed and asked me to stop questioning, I couldn't stop myself and I kept asking, "if that's the case why can't poor people who didn't have money just sit on the library and read them until they get sufficient knowledge, grow on their own and get a job without any marks?" She laughed at me and said, "hey look, these are good to talk but all of them are daydreams and it wouldn't work in practical life."   I couldn't speak anything because it was a new term I heard and I asked her, "what's a Practical life?" She said, "that is reality, my Mom always tells me to think practically." I was not sure what to think after that Mom, so tell me what exactly is practical life? After listening to this narration his mother understood that he's no longer a kid, he started to grow up. She felt a lot of thoughts before she could answer something and she said, "practical life is another word for what possibly happens and how everyone lives in a society my boy." For which the boy asked, "Mom if we didn't have any money to give this school where would I go to learn in this society? Where are the kids with less or no money going in this practical life?" Mother had no answers for his questions she asked him not to think of all these big stuffs and asked him to eat dinner and sleep soon. The kid slept off being tired but his mother couldn't sleep as his questions haunted her, she wanted to answer honestly but she couldn't find an answer that was convincing, also she was afraid of his growth and she was afraid if other kids would make him feel outcasted or whether he would go the wrong way. Thoughts went even deeper and his mother finally slept off after hours of tiring thoughts. She woke up the next morning also woke her son and said, "Son, there is only one life for everyone.

People who are not ready to accept the True purpose of being good and doing good to others, people who find difficult to be selfless, most importantly people who think of how others would think about their lives, are the ones always living a second life called "practical life." I don't want you to do that. Whatever questions you asked are for real and I really don't have convincing answers to judge that you were wrong too, but also I don't want you to stop thinking that way. You be a good kid, you study as much as you want, knowledge is learning and sharing it is not a race. Even if you are in a system where education is a competition, you don't have to rush and run, you just walk through it and make sure you learn anything that you like and want to learn. There is nobody who can scale or limit your knowledge with ranks, so I'm always here for you to support whatever you want to learn and do. So live a life that makes perfect sense to you, and keep questioning everything that doesn't make any sense." This conversation from his mother made him so convincing and liberated about his fearful speculation on whether his mother also wanted him to run as faster as all other parents expected from their kids. He smiled and kissed his mother's cheek and he happily got ready to go to school.

PRABHAT BHARDWAJ

FRAGRANCE OF LOVE

Almost a year and 2 months and 6 days of good friendship and an adorable relationship. I was going to meet her for the very first time. It was also the very first time in my life that I was meeting a stranger like this, although that stranger became my friend and now my love. Last evening I was preparing for her as usual like every boy does before meeting their partner. What to wear, hair should be in a managed way, trimmed beard, although I don't have full beard but still for grooming my self etc etc. and yess.... How can I forget my deo the best thing to apply on, you all are thinking about this , how can a deo be best thing to apply on. Don't worry , I will let you know a little later.

Our last call in the night was quite silent, so much to share with each other but the words shared was not exactly what we want to express, shortly she slept and it was only her breathe which could be heard at that time. The morning was so good , not so cold not so warm but still a little sunny day. Time was running and got nearer to the time when we were about to meet each other. How I was feeling at that time I can't express, happiness was on some another level, goosebumps were on loops, a lot of things are running inside me. May be that was the conversation between heart and mind where the soul was just listening silently and smiling. As she already told me many times that she doesn't know how to be late for anything or for anywhere she loves to be on time, but as usual I was late by 10-15 min, but that day I was late not because of my usual habit but because of the traffic and nothing else. She was waiting at the destination, standing with closed arms looking at the opposite side of the road , maybe she was looking at every auto and searching of me. And when I deboarded auto , I saw her and she silently turned her face with a little smile and change her standing position from front look to side look. She was in the same dress that I saw her for the first time on Facebook's profile pic. Looking so beautiful ,and innocent smile was making her cuter than she already is. I crossed the road went to her , "Hii kaisi ho"? I asked her, " dekh nhi rhe ho" she replied and start smiling with her small tongue out. I held both her arms and shook her a little bit. It was exactly like pinching yourself when you really don't know what happened surprisingly to you, and then I realized that finally, I am with her , I told her "I Love You", and " I know, isliye toh mil rahe hai"- she replied with her naughty smile. So I took the hall ticket and after sitting on our respective places, after passing 10-15 min , I spread my arms a little bit towards her so that she could put her hand into it and be comfortable. But she didn't , so I took her right hand and fixed it in my left hand while pulling her a little bit towards me, she was smiling and looking at me. Butterflies in the stomach and heartbeats were a little faster, maybe she was feeling the same, it was only 30min and her nails knocked my hand 4-5 times and then again I hold her hand with tangled fingers and told her "I Love You", be relaxed and comfortable.

After the interval, I took out the bracelet, my first gift to her and also it was the first thing which was a part of my preparation. I tied that bracelet to her and finally she hugged my arms and put her head on my shoulder and very firmly told me " I love you". After a while I put her face up by her chin and kissed her forehead and ran my finger on her face setting her hair beside her ear and kissed on her lips and her long breath I could feel that on my nose and cheek, that was the best feeling I had with her till that time. One of the amazing day of my life , Our first meeting , our first date , our first Valentine and our first kiss and that too on the kiss day.

It was an awesome feeling when I was returning to my home. I was so relaxed and firm that I took the window seat of the bus and lend my head and closed my eyes.All the moments were flashing and I was slightly smiling all the way and listening to the songs sent by her. I just stepped into my home and her call, " Ghar pahunch gaye"? "Yes" - I replied. "Ok! Aaj jaldi aa jana sone ke liye late mat karna" - She said. "Ok"- I replied. And as she wanted , I was early to bed and there, as in the morning she was waiting for me and we had a talk upon what happened the whole day , how she was feeling and what we had in our dinner , and at 12:00am, a whats app message , " You are my first Valentine , I don't know what destiny holds for us, but I will love you for my entire lifetime". And I replied- "Happy Valentine's day ,Jaana". She told me how much she liked my gift and I was looking nice in my black t-shirt. I replied all these things with "I Love You". And suddenly she told me - "You know I have not changed my top today after coming home." I asked - "Why so"? And here the answer what you people were left with in the starting why the deo was the best thing to apply on. So she replied - " Isme na tumhre deo ki fragrance aa rahi hai. And we both smiled.

SUHAN BANGERA

Rose

Oh! God, how could he do this to me I am visiting his house for the first time and he has not uttered a single line except for asking me to sit in is living room's sofa neither did he show himself for several minutes. I am the girl whom he had been dating for months I deserved his attention, it is the thing which I can rightfully demand from him. He had very well furnished house which clearly suggested he was no short in money but it was dead silent which was rather creepy and uncomfortable. After few minutes I had almost convinced myself that I was wrong about him these years and he is a rude narcissist. I know I was being silly but that time I felt my thoughts were well justified. When I was about to leave that place he entered room carrying a tray with two coffee mugs in it. "I am very sorry for keeping you waiting Bretta, my coffee machine broke down unexpectedly so I had to make coffee on my own", he said in a tone which had a perfect blend of apology and politeness. "It's OK Reed, it is very sweet that you made me coffee ", I said as politely as possible. His words made me to reconsider my thoughts. I started feeling that I judged him wrong. When he passed me a cup of coffee I stared into his eyes which were greenish blue in color coupled with a beautiful pair of eyebrows which made it, the most beautiful eyes I have ever seen and it suited him quite well. He was a horribly handsome guy, a tall fair stud with extremely good looks. He had a stunning personality and add on to it he had a successful and prosperous career as investment banker. He had always been polite and extremely caring towards me. He was seemingly a perfect guy. "You look gorgeous Bretta", he said while taking a sip of coffee. "Thanks, Even you are looking handsome Reed ,you always do", I took sip of coffee and I was not sure if it was because Reed made it or in fact it was the best coffee I had ever tasted. Reed and I spent next few minutes chatting with each other. His words were somewhat magical more I spoke to him more I felt he created illusion of paradise around me. Slowly we came close to each other and he gently placed his hand over my shoulders but suddenly at that moment the doorbell rang and Reed went to answer it. "Who the hell rang this doorbell?", I told to myself. Few moments later he came to me and said, "I am sorry Bretta it's my neighbor, he is a lonely old man and wants me to fix his bulb , it would take just 5 minutes only if you don't mind, may I?" I badly wanted to say, "YOU MAY NOT" but decided to maintain some civility so I said, "It's very sweet of you that you help your neighbors, you may go I won't mind". After Reed left, I expressed my excitement of starting a serious relationship with him. "Yes!, He is the perfect guy, everyone is gonna envy on me". After sometime when Reed didn't show up I decided to roam around his house, his house was well furnished and it had many rooms.   I noticed a shut room whose door was quite different from the rest. Curious to know what was stored in I opened the door. And I was quite surprised to see there were a lot of Mannequins inside, all of them were dressed neatly as a woman and wearing the wig which was unique to each mannequin and looked surprisingly natural. "Reed has a quite peculiar hobby, he never mentioned it to me" I explored that room all the mannequins were perfectly dressed they looked surprisingly natural, I don't know why but I started feeling a weird sense of discomfort and slight fear there, so I decided to move out of that place. As I came out one of the other rooms' door opened and a fair, tall and lean lady came out, she was almost of my age or probably younger. She was very beautiful and had a pair of dark black eyes with slight brownish tint which suited her well. She was just wearing a woolen top which raised above her knees somewhere between her thighs. I was shocked to see a girl in Reed's house even she looked terribly disappointed by my sight. She came to me and said, "What are you doing here?, Who are you?" "I am Bretta , Reed's girlfriend", I said though I was not sure about that status yet especially not after seeing her. "Who are you???", I added almost yelled at her. "I am Rose, Reed's... err.. sister", she replied. She looked around her and softly asked, "Where's Reed?". I sensed immense tension in her words. "He is out and will be back in few minutes" Suddenly her face adopted a lot more serious look and she said, "This is your chance, just get out of here and save yourself, GO" "What the hell are you saying??, Saving myself, why and from whom??" Once again she looked around to make sure no one else was present there. I realized she was afraid a lot. She said "From Reed. He is not the guy he seems to be, he is a psychopath a cold blooded serial killer. Initially he traps women like you then tortures them in most gruesome manner, in the way in which you cannot even imagine and then finally he will kill them and shave their head then creates a wig out of its hair, you have already seen those mannequins, haven't you? They are dressed as a replica of the women he killed and they wear the wigs he made out of the hair of his victims."   I was thunderstruck and was unable to decide whether to believe her or not. All the time I spent with Reed I always felt that he was a good man. At that moment I found it difficult to take a decision. Rose noticed my dilemma so she entered the room of mannequins and brought large book from there. It was a diary which contained descriptions and images of gruesomely mutilated dead women. I recognized the handwriting in the diary it was

Reed's. I felt terribly betrayed, a horrible sense of fear and anxiety ran over my thoughts "You have a chance go and save yourself, Run away", Rose said. I ran towards the door but when I opened it Reed was standing in front of me. "Where are going Bretta?", he said in his usual polite tone as he started moved towards me. I stepped back and was trying my best to not to look suspicious. Keeping a calm voice I said, " I.... I .. err...I got an important call, I need to go its urgent" "Why so hurry sweetheart it's hardy been an hour",he said then he gently placed his hands on my shoulder, "Darling just wait a little I have a huge surprise for you" . I would have felt this romantic before but now I felt disgust, I pushed him and stepped back, he noticed that I was carrying his diary he gave a devilish grin and said," Ok, you came to know about it, that's good at least you won't be surprised now" I tried to move out of his house forcefully but he grabbed hold of me and pushed me in so in my defense I punched his face hard and tried to repeat it again but he caught both of my hands and held me tightly in his arms he then whispered in my ears, "You have got some skills darling but well that won't save your skin today"

He pushed me and kicked my stomach I fell down crying with pain and cursing him. His grin became broader, the face which I felt handsome before now seemed to me like a thirsty vampire who was eager to suck my blood. But I got my hands on Reed's diary and with it I gave a hard blow to his head which knocked him down. Then I started running towards my car but before I could reach it, I felt dizziness, my sight started blurring out and my legs become too weak to hold me up. I fell down and started feeling suffocation "That damn coffee it was drugged", I yelled but I doubt if my voice came out of my vocal cord. I tried hard in vain to get up. I tried to call the cops but before I could dial anything Reed came there and crushed my phone.

He held my hand and dragged me in. I tried hard to resist but nothing yielded. "Learn to accept your fate Bretta, you can't escape. Told you already, your skills won't be saving your skin today", he said.   Reed slid his book shelf to open a hidden passage then he dragged me into it. It was dark inside, the only source of light there was, a dim bulb flickering at corner of the room. That room was stinking due to the presence of blood and rotten flesh which represented the savage nature of Reed. "What a brilliant aroma! I love this smell", Reed said. He then lifted me and tied my hands and neck to ropes which were already attached to the ceiling in a weird manner it was also connected to a system of pulleys. I was hung few feet above the ground .Due the affect of the drug I was unable to move. But although the rope was also tied to my neck it wasn't tight enough to choke me.   Reed then took a syringe filled with a colorless liquid and injected it to me. "This will undo the effect of the drug because I want you to cry, I want you to struggle, to move your body like a fish which is taken out of water, it pleasures me.", He said. "Just leave me Reed please", I cried and started to move my hands to and fro as an attempt to free myself but then I noticed the more I struggled more the rope around my neck tightened. I started losing all the hopes to survive so I started to move my body as an attempt choke and kill myself which I felt was better than Reed's tortures. Reed gave a devilish laugh "Trying to kill yourself?, I know better dear, I have designed this system, no matter how much you try, it won't kill you at least not before I kill you". I never was this desperate before, I started crying loudly "Why are you doing this?, What do you get out of this Reed?....... WHAT?" "Because it gives me peace dear, I never heard a sound more pleasing than a cry of a woman", Reed said while he was playing with different kinds of knives "You know dear, I was born in an orphanage to a teenage girl, she died as soon as I was born. I grew up in an orphanage where everyone said I am different, my thoughts are different. I was called Alastor. Always either they kept distance from me or when in group they abused me, tortured me until one day I ran away from there. I worked hard earned lot of money grew up to this level but all this day to day activities used to frustrate me...bore me, I needed a better reason to live so I started nurturing my childhood hobby, my passion that is seeing people in pain especially women. You know nothing can be more satisfying than the sight of blood but the point is no one realizes it". "Oh, god help me", I cried. "You are a F***** demon". "Naah, I am ALASTOR",he said rather proudly. Then he took a surgeon's knife and came near me " I am supposed to give a goodbye present". He gently placed surgeon's knife in the region just below my collar bone then gradually started applying pressure to it and then suddenly he made a deep cut on that region. "AHH...!!",I cried with pain. "That was pleasing, now let me give you my autograph",he said and started writing the name Alastor on my wrist using the surgeon's knife. I could see the deep scarlet blood dripping from my wound. "No, don't do it, for the god's sake please Reed NO" , I said and then closed my eyes and screamed insanely. Gradually I started losing my consciousness but then all of a sudden I heard a gun shot and Reed stopped. I slowly opened my eyes and saw that Reed was lying dead on the floor, he was shot on the head. An old man was standing in front of me, he was carrying a vintage rifle in his hand. He untied the ropes and freed me. Probably because of the wound and mental strain I fell unconscious. When I had regained my consciousness I was lying on a bed, my wounds were dressed and that old man was sitting in front of me he was reading Reed's diary and muttering,"Jesus!, This man's a devil, its good he is gone now". I noticed that, old man's eyes were wet suggesting he was crying. "Where am I ?",I said. "Thank god you woke up I am relieved now, don't worry you are safe here it's my house. I am a Doctor, Dr Rick Adler. Feel comfortable and take rest, I will get you soup.", old man said and moved out of the room. "It was a horrible nightmare, I wish it was just that", I told myself but now there was something else which was bothering me. I was wondering who Rose was, Reed said that he was an orphan, which clearly meant Rose could not be his sister. Moreover I even didn't know that where she was now. The old man entered the room with the bowl of hot soup, he gave it to me and said, "My bulb was not working properly so I called Reed to help me up to fix it, but when he came to my house he told me that my bulb had completely burnt out and it cannot be used. He asked me to wait for a while until he brings a spare bulb from his house but when he didn't show himself for several minutes, I went to his house and there I heard your cries , so I tried to call cops but the network is down all over this place, which forced me to take the matter on my own hands. I brought my rifle and as you know the rest is a history". "Thank you sir, thanks a lot you saved my life I don't know how can I repay your debt", I said "Hey, no need to repay anything, as a human I did what I was supposed to do and moreover you remind me of my granddaughter". "Your granddaughter? , where's she now?" He became silent for a moment and then took a deep breath and said,"She ran away from here, couple of years ago to lead an independent life, I never heard of her since then..........Until today." He then opened Reed's diary and passed it to me "It's my granddaughter". I was thunderstruck when I saw it. It was the picture of a terribly mutilated corpse of the same woman whom I had met at Reed's house. It was Rose's corpse!!

THE END (or is it?)

HINDI POEMS

<u>WASIQUE AZIZ</u>

<u>हिंद का हूँ मैं बाशिंदा</u>

हिंद का हूँ मैं बाशिंदा,
दिनकर की मैं वाणी हूँ ,
शायरों का मैं चाहने वाला,
पंत की जवानी हूँ।
गालिब का हूँ चौङ मैं ,
अल्लामा का इकबाल हूं,
सूर्यकांत सा निराला
हरिवंश की मधुशाला।
टैगोर की गीतांजलि मैं ,
अहमद का फ़राज़ हूँ ,
कबीर सा मशहूर हूँ मैं ,
इलिया सा बदनाम हूँ।
राहत सा बेखौफ हूँ मैं ,
मुनव्वर का जज़्बात हूँ ,
वाजपेयी सा अटल हूँ मैं
तुलसी का मैं दास हूँ।
और, कृष्ण का उपदेश हुं मैं ,
मुहम्मद का पैगाम हूँ ,
हिंद का हूँ मैं बशिंदा,
मुकम्मल हिंदुस्तान हूँ।

BHUMIJA SINGH

वाकिफ हूँ।

वो रोज़ रात देर तक जागने से वाकिफ हूँ
बेवजह के खयालों में खोए रहने से वाकिफ हूँ
भीड़ से दूर तन्हा रहने से वाकिफ हूँ
अंधेरे में खुद को बंद कर गाना सुनने से वाकिफ हूँ
आखिर पेशे से मैं भी आशिक हूँ
टूटे हुए हर दिल से वाकिफ हूँ।

ANJALI PATHAK

जिंदगी

ऐ जिंदगी अब तू रूकना नहीं।
तू नदी सा बन और बहता चला चल,
इस दहकती धूप में कभी सूखना नहीं,
ऐ जिंदगी अब तू रूकना नहीं।
बेशक ठोकर मिलेंगे रास्ते पर,
पर तू उनसे टकराकर लुढ़कना नहीं,
ऐ जिंदगी अब तू रूकना नहीं।
माना कि सिर पर जिम्मेदारियों का भार है,
और उस पर कष्ट भी करता प्रहार है,
पर तू उसके बोझ तले झुकना नहीं,
ऐ जिंदगी अब तू रूकना नहीं।
तू आईना तो बन,
पर सिर्फ दुसरो की असलियत दिखाने को,
तू कांच की भांति कभी टूटना नहीं,
ऐ जिंदगी अब तू रूकना नहीं।
रास्ता थोड़ा लम्बा है,
मंजिल अभी आगे है,
और रास्ते में बिखरे उलझनों के कई धागे हैं,
पर तू उनमें उलझकर उलझना नहीं,
ऐ जिंदगी अब तू रूकना नहीं।
ऐ जिंदगी तूझसे बस इतनी ही गुज़ारिश है,
रफ़्तार जो तूने पकड़ी है,
उसे कभी छोड़ना नहीं,
अपना रूख पिछे की ओर कभी मोड़ना नहीं,
अगर मिले कभी रास्ते पर मुसिबतो का पहाड़,

तो तू डर कर उसके पिछे छुपना नहीं,
ऐ जिंदगी अब तू रूकना नहीं।

AYUSHI RANI

अनोखा धोखा-

दुनिया का दस्तूर अनोखा,
हम जो देखे है सब धोखा।
प्रेम अनोखा तबसे है,
जबसे है मेहसूस किया,
पग लाख मारा है हमने,
प्रणय हमेशा है पाया।
दुनिया का दस्तूर अनोखा,
हम जो देखे है सब धोखा।
आंचल में सम्भाला है,
चलना उसने सिखाया है,
गिर जो आए सीने से लगया है,
सही गलत का मोल उसने सिखाया है।
दुनिया का दस्तूर अनोखा,
हम जो देखे है सब धोखा।
अपना जिन्हें बनाया है,
ऋतु सा रंग बदला हैं,
नाकार जिन्हें हम आए है,
आभर उन्होनें दिखाए है।
दुनिया का दस्तूर अनोखा,
हम जो देखे है सब धोखा।
अफताब की अग्नि ने,
मुखड़े अनेक जलाए है,
फ़तह की ऊँचाई ने,
याराना कितने गिराए है।

दुनिया का दस्तूर अनोखा,
हम जो देखे है सब धोखा।

ALOK PATHAK

अधूरे सपने

यादें जहन में उसकी अब भी बाकी हैं
निकली थी घर से वो चहकती हुई
रोज की तरह हंसती-हसाती हुई
सोचा था उसने करना कुछ नया सा है
बदलना इतिहास था आज जो पुराना सा है
कंधों पर बस्ता अपना लिए
निकली थी घर से वो इक सपना लिए
वापस घर को जब आऊंगी
खुशखबरी मैं मां को पहले सुनाऊंगी
उन बेपरवाह सपनों की सांसें   अब भी बाकी हैं
यादें जहन में उसकी अब भी बाकी हैं।

उम्मीदों के अथाह सागर पर पुल हौसले से अपने बनाना था
बेटियां कतई बेटों से कम नहीं
जमाने को उसने यह दिखलाना था
हौसलों से भरी गई वह इम्तिहान देने
मिल गई थी राह उसको
जिस पर चलने का देखा था सपना उसने
अचानक पलट गया उसका संसार
जब कुछ स्वान चरित्र भेड़ियों ने
कर दी अपनी हदें पार
हजम कर गए उसकी आबरू को
अपना निवाला समझकर
कर दी इज्जत उसकी तार-तार

पल भर में चूर हुए उन सपनों की सिसक
अब भी बाकी हैं
यादें जहन में उसकी अब भी बाकी हैं।

फेंक कर अधमरा छोड़ चले गए
क्या तब भी उनकी आत्मा रोयी नहीं
एक जीवित लौ को बुझा गए
क्या तब भी उनकी कामना सोई नहीं
मां कैसे यह उधड़ा शरीर देखेगी
वो यही सोची होगी
लगाई छत से छलांग उसने
ना जाने कितनी बार वह तड़पी होगी।

नसों को चीर दो उनकी
नजरें उठाए जो नारी की तोहीन कर
प्रण लो जो सामने ऐसा कुकृत्य दिखेगा
दोबारा कोई सोचे ना करने की हरकत ऐसी
कसम धरती मां की
गाड़ देंगे उसको जमीन पर।

जब तक खत्म ना होगी दहशत इनकी
समाज में बढ़ती रहेगी वहशत इनकी
पूरे ना होंगे उसके सपने
जिसकी घर लौट आने की आस अभी बाकी है।

यादें जेहन में उसकी अब भी बाकी हैं
यादें जेहन में उसकी अब भी बाकी हैं।

ABHAY SONI

वो तो रूठ गयी मुझसे

अरे वो तो रूठ गयी मुझसे,
सोचा था आज फिर दिल उनके नाम कर दूं,
चलो कोशिशें करता हूँ,
उनके दिल में उस घर को ढूंढने की,जहां रहा करता था इश्क़ मेरा,
पर वो तो रूठ गयी मुझसे,
चलो कोशिशें करता हूँ,
उनके रूह में उस एहसास को ढूंढने की जहां कभी मेरा इश्क़ मुक्कमल था।
पर वो तो रूठ गयी मुझसे,
चलो कोशिशें करता हूँ,
उनके उन नखरों को खोजने की जो सिर्फ मुझसे अपनी नुमाइशें पूरी कराता
था

पर वो तो रूठ गयी मुझसे,
पर वो तो रूठ गयी मुझसे।।

वो इश्क़ ही तो था

वो इश्क़ ही तो था जो मुझे तो तुम्हारी ओर ले आया,
वो इश्क़ ही तो था जो मुझे पागल सा कर गया।
तुम्हारी इश्क़ की मदहोशी में कुछ इस कदर डूबे,
न होना था एक जानते हुए भी तुझमें खुद को खोये।
वो इश्क़ ही तो था जो मैं तुझमें खोया,
वो इश्क़ ही तो था जो मुझे पागल सा कर गया।
क्यूं हुई मोहहबत इस कदर जब हम दोनों का मुक़्क़द्दर एक न था,
क्यूँ हुई मोहहबत इस कदर जब मेरा नसीब ही तुझसे जुड़ा न था।
वो इश्क़ ही तो था जो मुझे पागल सा कर गया,
वो इश्क़ ही तो था जो मुझे पागल सा कर गया।

POOJA VAISHNAV

<u>पिता</u>

आज कल के इस मतलबी दुनिया मे कौन किसी का होता है,
बेवजह बेहिसाब प्यार करने वाला एक बाप ही तो होता है...

हमे तो वो दिन याद नहीं पापा हम तो बहुत छोटे थे,
जब हमे सूखे मे सुलाकर खुद गीले मे सो जाया करते थे...

याद है वो दिन जब हम स्कूल जाने से कतराते थे,
आप बड़े प्यार से स्कूल छोड़ने टॉफ़ीयां लेकर जाया करते थे...

भूल जाती थी पापा आपके उन एहसानो को,, जब आप फटे
कपड़े पहनकर हमे महंगे कपड़े दिलाते थे,
काश वो पल वही थम जाता जब आप मुझे अपने हाथों से
खाना खिलाते थे...

बहुत याद आते हैं पापा वो पल जब मै देर रात तक पढ़ती थी
तो आप भी जागते थे,
काश वो पल वही थम जाता जब आप मुझे लोरियाँ सुनाते थे...

आपने मुझे हमेशा सही और गलत मे फैसला करना सिखाया,
जहां मुझे आपकी जरूरत थी मैंने हमेशा आपको वाहा पाया..

सपने देखना मुझे आपने सिखाया, कांटो भरी राह पर चलना मुझे आपने
सिखाया,
दुनिया के लोगों की पहचान करना आपने ही तो बतलाया..

आपने मुझे हमेशा एक बेटे की तरह आज़ादी दी,
क्यु मै भूल जाती थी मै आपकी ही तो शहजादी थी..

बड़ी खुशी मिलती है जब लोग मुझे आपके नाम से जानते हैं,
बेटी बिल्कुल बाप पे गई है ऐसा लोग मानते हैं...
क्यु गए कलकत्ता आप, अगर आप वहाँ न जाते तो शायद ऐसा होता
नहीं,
एक बेटी के सर से पिता का साया खोता नहीं..

जाते वक्त पापा आपने हमे जरूर पुकारा होगा, जरूर याद किया होगा,
हर वक्त, हर पल ये गम ये अफसोस रहेगा हमे जब आपने
हमारी यादों मे आख़री साँस लिया होगा...

काश हम आपके आखिर वक्त मे भी आपके साथ होते,
पर शायद खुदा को ये मंजूर न था वरना हम आपका साथ कभी न
खोते..

हर वक्त, हर पल मेरी माँ आपकी यादों मे रोती है
क्यु चले गए मेरी माँ को यूँ छोड़कर
अब तो वो रातों में भी चैन से ना सोती है...

मेरी लाख गलतियों पर पर्दा डाला आपने,
मेरी हर ख्वाहिशो को पूरा किया आपने,
क्यु चले गए हमे बीच मजधार मे यूं छोड़कर
क्यु बेबस और लाचार बना दिया हमे आपने...

हमे नहीं चाहिये ये दौलते शौहरतें,
हमे तो बस आपकी जरूरत है,
हम झोपड़ी में रह लेते, रूखी सुखी रोटियां खा लेते,
पर पापा हमे तो बस आपके साथ की जरूरत है...

आप तो कुदरत का वो तौफा हो जो भुलाए नहीं भूलता,
क्या लिखूँ पापा मै आपके लिए आपकी यादें मिटाए नहीं मिटता...

लाख कोशिशें कर लूँ पापा आपको पाने की, पर ये शायद मुमकिन
नहीं,
पर छीन लाऊ आपको उस रब से ये भी शायद मुमकिन नहीं...

अगर बस मेरा चले तो छीन लाऊ आपको उस रब से,
मेरी आँखे तरस गई है आपको देखने को कब से

आपकी यादों को कितना रोकु पापा ये रुकता नहीं,
ये तो आपके प्यार का वो तौफा है जो लुटता नहीं...

पिता है तो अभिमान है,
पिता है तो रोटी कपड़ा मकान है,
पिता नहीं तो सुना ये जहाँन है...

तु मेरा पहला प्यार

मै तेरे आँखो मे डूब जाती थी, तु मुझे प्यार भरी नज़रों से देखता था,
तु उस वक्त मेरा पहला प्यार हुआ करता था..

मै हर पल तेरा इंतज़ार किया करती थी, तेरे इश्क़ का दीदार किया
करती थी,
तु ही तो था जिसकी मै परवाह किया करती थी..

दर ब दर फिरता था तु मुझमें जैसे तेरे इश्क़ का फितूर मुझमें चढ़ जाता
था, तेरे ख्वाबों के बगैर कम्बख्त नींद भी कहा आता था...

मै परछाइ बन हर सफर में तेरे साथ चला करती थी,
वो तु ही तो था जिससे मैं बेपनाह मोहब्बत किया करती थी..

कौन था मेरा? एक तु ही तो था जो मेरी साँसों में बसा हुआ था
तु मेरी जरूरत मेरी चाहत हुआ करता था..

मै तुझे महसूस किया करती थी, तेरी आहट मुझे छू कर गुजर जाया
करती थी,
वो तु ही था जो मेरे इतने करीब था...

जब तुझसे नज़रें मिलती थी, मै होश में भी बेहोश हुआ करती थी,
वो तु ही था जो मेरा नशा हुआ करता था..

झूठे थे वो तेरे आँशु और तेरे वादे भी झूठे थे,
तु उस वक्त झूठे ख्वाब दिखाया करता था...

तु मेरी आदत हुआ करता था मेरी इबादत हुआ करता था,
तु मेरी चाहत का गलत फायदा उठाया करता था..

तु रूठता था, मै मनाती थी, पर तु मुझे नज़रअंदाज़ किया करता था,
तु वो था जो मेरे प्यार की कभी कद्र ही नहीं किया करता था

तु कभी अपने दुखों की नुमाइश करता था,
मै सुनती थी समझती थी, तेरे आँशु पोछःती थी,
पर तु मुझे सिर्फ दुखों मे ही याद किया करता था...

***

NITESH MANDAL

अगर मुझे इश्क़ दुबारा हो गया!!

देखो उजाले का रंग काला हो गया,
ऐ चाँद..तू हर रात क्यों घर से बाहर निकल आता है..
क्या तू भी मेरी तरह आंवारा हो गया?
कुछ ख़्वाब आ रहे थे हक़ीक़त से रूबरू होने..
लौट गए रास्ते से ये कहकर.
.कि चलो अब काफी अंधियारा हो गया,
और मैंने थोड़ी देर उस सितारे से मुँह क्या मोड़ा..
वो औरों के साथ इतनी खूबसूरती से उलझा कि मुझसे ही पराया हो
गया,

मेरे आंसुओ को देरी होने लगी है अब आंखों तक आने में..
क्या उनके रास्ते भी अब घर तुम्हारा हो गया?
और अब तुम्हें नहीं..
.बस तुम्हारा ना होना मांगता हूँ खुदा से,
क्योंकि अश्क़ लाल हो जाएंगे मेरे अब
अगर मुझे इश्क़ दुबारा हो गया!!

****

92

NISHAT USMANI

इश्क

तेरा ये इश्क मुझे अब फरेब सा लगता है ,
तू हवस को ही शायद इश्क समझता है !
हमारा इश्क तो मुरझाए उस गुलाब सा है ,
सूखने के बावजूद जो अपने वजूद में रहता है !

✳ ✳ ✳

MAST MAIKAASH

शाम जवाँ हुई,

शाम जवाँ हुई,
रात ने उफान लिया, अंगड़ाई का।
रात भर एक दूसरे को समझते रहे।
रात भर ककहरे सिखाये एक दूजे को हमने।
रात भर लैब चलती रही इश्क़ की।
दिल मसलते रहे, जिस्म चलते रहे,
दोनों ने बुझाई आग राख डाल कर,
फिर भी वक़्त क़त्ल हुआ सारी रात।
एक बात समझ आयी वैसे रात को भी,
जब जलन हो, आग और पानी में दोनों के,
तो बुझाये ना बुझेगी दावानल की गर्मी।
दोनों थक के जब अलग हुए एक पल को,
साँसे साँसों में भरकर ही आहें चलीं।
बोझिल हुई पलकें जब देर रात,
दोनो थक कर लिपट जब सोने चले।
यूँ लगा ये असाइनमेंट जैसे पूरा हुआ हो अब।
सुबह देखा तो बिस्तर खाली पड़ा था, काजल,

बिंदी, थोड़ी लाली, मनटीका पड़ा था।

रात कोने में पड़ी हांफती ही रही थी,
बिस्तर की सलवटें जो वाकिफ थीं हर बात से,
चुपचाप लगीं थी समेटने में खुद को।
बाद में दिन ने ये मुखबिरी में बताया,
कल मोहब्बत ने इम्तेहान के बाबत,
दिल से बिस्तर का सफर किया था।
थ्योरी में तो क्या ही मजा आना था, इसलिए,
रात भर लैब चलती रही इश्क़ की।

<u>बड़ी देर से नाराज बैठे हैं</u>

बड़ी देर से नाराज बैठे हैं नाज़नीन हमसे।
दूर जाकर उस अंधेरे कमरे में,
जहां दिन के उजाले में भी जाएं कभी,
तो हाथ थाम कर पीछे चलते थे,आहिस्ता आहिस्ता से।
बड़े मासूम से थे वो पल,वो चेहरे।
वो बोलें ना सही पर चाहते तो होंगे ही,
कि आऊँ मैं दीवाने की तरह और हाथ थाम कर,
धीमे से होंठ चूम लूँ।
पीछे हटना फिर जैसे उनका मंज़ूर करना हो।
होंठो पर चुंबन फिर उधर से आये,
गर्मियों के मौसम की लूह में बही,
बाग के पत्तों के झूरमुटों से सरकी,
ठंडी एक बयार के जैसे!
इजाजत मिल जाये, कि
जाओ! माफीनामा है ये,जानकारी छाप दो,
दोनों दिलों के अखबारों में,
बड़े दिन बाद सबको सुर्खियां मिली हैं।
-'मस्त' मैकश

***

PANKAJ SAHU

उनका दीदार

सिर्फ़ काजल से ही उनका पूरा श्रृंगार होता है,
फिर भी ईद के चांद की तरह उनका दीदार होता है।
हुस्न ऐसा की हर रोज़ मेरी नियत का इम्तिहान होता है,
फिर भी ईद के चांद की तरह उनका इंतेज़ार होता है।
सोचा था आसान होगा राह-ए-इश्क़ पर चलना,
पर यहाँ तो हर मोड़ पर उनके आशिक़ों से तकरार होता है,
फ़िर भी ईद के चांद की तरह उनका दीदार होता है।

SONU SUMAN

मैं दिल का बुरा नहीं साहब

दिल का बुरा नहीं हूँ साहब,
थोड़ा सौदेबाजी में कच्चा हूँ ...
तोलता नहीं रिश्तों को पैसे के तराजू में,
इसलिए खुदगर्जी की नजरों में सीधा सादा हूँ....
नहीं फिसलती नजरें हर एक चेहरे पे,
इसलिए थोड़ा दुनिया की दौड़ से पीछे हूँ...
नहीं लगा कर घूमता चेहरे पर नक़ाब साहब,
शायद इसलिए लोगों की भीड़ में अकेला हूँ...
बार बार नकारा है मेरे आँसुओं को चकाचौन्द वाली रोशनी में,
मैं सुबह का भरोशा नहीं, अंधेरो का भी साथी हूँ..
. मैं दिल का बुरा नहीं साहब, बस थोड़ा सौदेबाज़ी में कच्चा हूँ...

*** * ***

<u>अगर न हो तुझे.....</u>

अगर न हो तुझे, तेरी खूबसूरती पर यकीन,
तो अपनी बेइंतहा खूबसूरती मेरी आँखों मे देख लेना....
अगर कम हो भरोशा खुद पर कभी,
तो मेरी आँखों के गुरुर की वजह में खुद को ढूंढ लेना....
शायद अल्फाज़ो में बयान न कर पाऊं अहमियत तेरी,
लेक़िन तुझे खोने के डर को,
मेरी रातों को खुली हुई आँखों में देख लेना....
बनाया है ख़ुदा है ने तुझे, अपने सबसे ख़ास हुनर से..
अगर न हो फिर भी यक़ीन,
तो मेरी हर इबादत में, तेरे नाम की गूंज को पहचान लेना...

SHASHANK SHEKHAR

वह!

मेरी रूह से होकर गुजरती है वह,
सांसे थम सी जाती हैं जब मुझे छूकर गुजरती है वह।
मैं समझ नहीं पाया मगर,
कुछ तो खास है उसमें,
एक अजीब सा अहसास है उसमें,
उससे मिलकर ऐसा लगता है मानो छुपे गई राज हैं उममें।
जिंदगी को बहुत बारीकी से जीती है वह ,
(कहते हैं ना हर लम्हे का लुफ्त उठाना) बस ऐसा ही करती है वह,
हर लम्हे को खुल के जीती है वह।
सब कहते हैं बहुत अजीब है वह,
सच तो वही जानते हैं जिनके करीब है वह,
जिस मां ने उसे जन्म दिया उस मां का प्यारा नसीब है वह।
सपने कुछ ज्यादा बड़े नहीं हैं उसके बस दुनिया में प्यार बांटना चाहती है,
उसे फर्क नहीं पड़ता इस बात से पीठ पीछे उसे दुनिया क्या बुलाती है,
वह तो बस हर किसी का गम बांट कर हर किसी के चेहरे पर खुशी लाना
चाहती है।।

SALONI SHARMA

#इश्क़!!

नाम तो सुना ही होगा आज इसके पैग़ाम सुनाती हूँ..
इश्क़ वो नहीं जो झुकाना चाहे,
इश्क़ तो वो है जो हर बार तेरे लिए झुक जाए।।
इश्क़ की आस नहीं के हासिल जीत हो,
इश्क़ तो वो है जो हार कर भी प्यार हासिल कर जाए।।
इश्क़ ये भी नहीं के इसमें कोई बंदिशें रखे,
इश्क़ तो वो है जो खुले दिल से आसमा तक पहुँचा जाए।।
इश्क़ वो नहीं जो आपसे गुनाह कराए,
इश्क़ तो वो है जो आपके हर गुनाह को माफ़ कर जाए।।
इश्क़ में ना होते कोई सौदे है,
इश्क़ तो वो है जिसमें कुर्बान हर चाहत हो जाए।।
इश्क़ ऐसा नहीं के रिश्तों में रंजिशें हो,
इश्क़ तो वो है जिसमें मनाना ही प्यार जताना हो जाए।।
इश्क़ मंज़िल की उम्मीद दिलाए ज़रूरी नहीं,
इश्क़ तो वो है जो हर सफ़र साथ जी जाए।।
इश्क़ में कोई किसी की आद्त न बने,
इश्क़ तो वो है जो हर इबाद्त में पुकारा जाए।।
इश्क़ आंकता नहीं तालीम किसी की,
इश्क़ तो वो है जो हर तहज़ीब को हो जाए।।

❋ ❋ ❋

इश्क़ हो तो कैसा हो..!!

ख्वाइश की इश्क़ का निखार कुछ ऐसा हो,
जैसे राधा को कान्हा के मोह ने साधा हो।।
छोड़ जाती है परछाइयाँ भी साथ अंधेरे में,
पर तेरा साथ तो फ़लक के भी उस पार तक हो।।
ख़्वाब तो ऐसे कई आते है हर रात बिन बात,
मगर शर्त है इश्क़ में के इनमें भी सूरत सिर्फ तेरी हो।।
जैसे तिनका तिनका पंछी अपनी शाला बनाते है न,
बस वैसा ही एक अपना छोटा सा प्यार का आशियाना हो।।
देखा है ललक मुसाफिरों की मंज़िल तलाशते हुए,
इल्तेज़ा है इतनी सी के इश्क़ की चाहत भी इसकदर तृषित हो।।
जैसे फिजाएँ चलती है मदमस्त अन्नत तक,
कुछ ऐसी ही इश्क़ की बुनियाद शाश्वत तक बेबाक हो।।
देखे बिना कृष्ण को मीरा अधूरी तो नहीं,
पर बेशक़ अरदासे उसकी श्यामल के एक झलक से ही पूरी हो।।
यूँ तो किसी को बे-सबब हक़ अदा न करूँ,
पर इश्क़ जो तुझसे करूँ तो ताउम्र तक़दार तुम्ही हो।।

✳ ✳ ✳

CO-AUTHORS

I *am Prabeer Deepak, Currently working in* SANY *heavy industries,* India. I *have a desire to learn and the pen is that weapon which fulfills that desire. Highly optimistic person with the vision to curate things with* Perfection.

Sani Hossain, a 21 years young passionate, enthusiastic, enigmatic dedicated Writer, Blogger, a crazy Soccer player, dreams to be a Professor & profound Writer. Hailed from Hatinagar, a small village in Berhampore,Murshidabad of West Bengal, pursuing Literature in English at College of Osmania University, Hyderabad. Esoteric & Aesthetic Being, Loves writing Romantic,Emotional,Didactic genres. He's so funny, jovial,charming, understanding & amiable.And can stay in touch with his Insta Id: (Sherr.s.sani). Facebook~ Sani Sh. Blog~ www.esotericsani.blogspot.com

I *am Pooja-Trivedi Raval. My pen name is* SMIT. I *know almost 16 Foreign languages. I like to train people for the same. I love to evolve my emmotions on paper. I am from Ahmedabad.*

Swati Mishra is a graduation student .She loves to write and express deep visions .

Don't tell me the moon is shining; show me the glint of light on broken glass. A professional writer is an amateur who didn't quit. physiotherapist by profession writer by default

I am Riya Das, a writer and poet. Expelling some of my pain through my words. IG - @the_humming_moon

Freya Shah is a science student. She tries to spread the meaning of love through her pen. She loves to write. Her happiness is hidden in others smile

My name is Anirudh, an aspiring writer love to travel along with emotions. Exploring emotions through characters, tales, poems and all forms of art and literature is my collective evolution process.

Gopi Manoj is a 22-year old Indian author who debuted with his book "The Truth Can't Be Hidden: The Secret of Akhel Caves". He is a software engineer working in TCS at Banglore. He aims to write in simple English which can be understood by all ages of people. He likes writing adventures and science fiction novels. Currently he is busy with his second book about his experiences at kerala and anthologies with the support of his friend Roy.

I'm a management student with a passionate writer, i love writing about life's ups and downs, poems and stories. I believe in self motivation and to self energetic to improve yourself instead of others.

Pankaj Sahu
Writer & philosopher

An artist with a soul of feelings who bleeds words of emotions so one can lost themself in this paradise. And write for everyone that can relate and heal themselves.

The author is a computer science undergraduate and has interests in regional literature, cultural development, contemporary politics and technological advances.

An Engineer by profession.A writer, historian,science lover by passion. complex from inside but simple from outside. Loves to write in Hindi and Urdu.
A plain open book for all.

Tarun Jeevnani is a business owner in bhopal.
He has completed his engineering from S.I.R.T. college, bhopal.
He likes to read but has never written anything on his own this is the second anthology in which he has taken part in.

Experienced content writer and a former sub-editor, who quit her job as a software engineer to pursue her passion for writing. She writes about everything, be it love, sports, technology, bikes, cars, or marketing. Apart from writing, she loves reading and travelling. Follow her on instagram at @thesoulbite.

She is 20 year girl ,studuies at marwari girls collage ranchi, writing gives her pleasure and reducess all the sorrows.... writing gives ladder of hope to deals with situation and problem.for more write-up visit her yourquote profile Nishat Usmani or insta page nisu_nishat26..

I am a teacher, poet and youtuber. I uploades my poetry videos in my YouTube channel named Anjali Pathak.

My name is Shashank Shekhar.
Currently I'm persuing B.Sc (HONS)
Agriculture.
Hobbies are playing football and participate in
different sports.

Myself Sumegha from garden city if
Karnataka completed masters currently
enjoying the Motherhood, I am very much
interested in writing and reading quotes
especially on life and experience.

I am an aspiring actor, poet &
storyteller. As far as writing is concerned
I don't tell that I write well enough but
for posting my write-ups I have a page on
Instagram named "heartwhispers07".

Dhiraj Arora is a writer in making, he is from Nagpur, Maharashtra, India. He has written some poems and stories as well. Beside this he is a businessman also. His instagram id is @dhiru_01 He loves to follow his passion and live life to fullest.

Name Given As Sonu Suman. Born on 8th June 1992. Techie by profession And a writer by Heart. Just trying to write the experiences into words given by life.

Nickunj Joshi is a 24 year old accounting professional.He hails from the town of Gandhidham kutch in Gujarat. A humble guy who expresses himself in both words and actions, understanding, loyalty is his policy.he can impress anyone by his words.for his write up instagram @nj__wriTes.

Sanjana Nudurupati is a 19 year old aspiring writer from Hyderabad, currently pursuing Bachelor's degree in engineering from CMREC, Medchal.

Priya V. Vaswani
Nagpurian
Graduated Pharmacy professional
Pursuing M. Pharm
Pen name/ Insta activity handle :
@pandawrites14
E mail - priyavaswan5@gmail.com

Dimple Gehani is an Author, quote writer, poetess and an interior designer
Her debut book was launched in july 2019 named "Shiny feelings (say yes to the feelings)" before that she was a writer in many anthologies..

She also handles an active instagram page
being__writer

Belongs to a small village in
Deoghar,Jharkhand.
Completed Bachelor's degree in maths from
St. Xavier's College, Ranchi.
Started writing at an early age but still not
a professional one.
Can follow my writings on Instagram
@poetriotic_insta .

Utkanth Vasoya is is an
Entrepreneur, Investor ,
Writer , author and Blogger
And having a influencing
personality.

A 19 year old boy from Belgaum,
who began to write his heart out.
For all he believed that poetry
would create magic.

BURHANUDDIN ABDEALI SHAYAR Born on 08 december 2000. He had studied in madresah Taiyebiyah english medium senior secondary school partapur.He is doing his graduation from pune phuley university. His passion is his dignity. His love towards poems shows his strong feelings , happiness , emotion and strong perfection of virtues . He have achieved many certificates for his success

Basically an engineering student but loves stories more than anything else, my love for stories is the reason why ended up writing stories. Along with literature I am a martial arts and fitness enthusiast.
At present I write short stories but also preparing for my debut novel.

I'm Mohammed Umar M from Bangalore currently working and I love to read, write and during free time I cook as well so I love to play football and my I'd is @poetry_makers

पंकज सा शोभित मानस पटल पर
वर्णनातित प्रकाश पुंज हूं
मैं भेड़ियों का शोर नहीं
गरजते शेर की गूंज हूं

रांची का रहने वाला और नाम मेरा आलोक पाठक है।

I'm approachable , sweet and kind depends on you .
Tactful , Zealous , Diplomatic.
Obviously oblivious at stages.
I'm fond of facades because they were once considered to precious things like you and your positive side which was the only thing that felt real.

Just a merry child of the universe, rolling in it's creases and painting stars, watered by rill of words and lead by heart.

I am an aspiring poet. I am just trying my best to make people read what i write.

My name is pooja vaishnav my father's name is Mr. Akhikesh vaishnav and my mother's name is Mrs. Yashoda Vaishnav I'm 21year old, I'm from raipur chhattisgarh I'm BSc graduate in 2019 from govt Nagarjuna science collage raipur and now I'm a MSc mathematics student from Mats University..

I'm a 15 year old guy who is passionate about writing short stories and poems. I am much interested in Music too.

Saeraa.S is her pen name, lives in Pune and is currently pursuing degree in Mechanical Engineering. She's an animal lover, likes to read suspense and write on philosophy. Her interests is to study animal psychology. Night sky and nature are her inspiration. Believes in karma.
Instagram handle - the.soultalks

This is SHAHREEN KAHKASHA.
Pursuing bio.tech . I threw out my inner feels through my tales. I wrote for fun. I run a personal Blog on Instagram as @unrivalled_thoughts , where I share all my inner thoughts.

Simran Nishchal is 17 yrs old, a 12th standard student from Delhi.
She loves to pen down her thoughts. Her goal is to become a makeup artist.
You can get connected to her through her Instagram handle :-
@thatinsomniacwriter

I'm Shruti Singh from the city of nawabs lucknow Utter pradesh .
Currently I am a student and from past 1 year i 've been writing .
I think their are so many unsaid words in this beautiful life ,i just feel and observe them and frame in form of poetries and quotes.

I'm just a dreamer, unsupervised,
Within a world of eyes,
Fighting for what lies beyond appearances;
Trying to find my way to somewhere I belong.

Akshat Dixit is a upcoming writer from Lucknow currently pursuing BBA from Dehradun.A lover of Art and poetry.You can contact him on Instagram @bitterstillsweet

I ,S K Nandhini born in Karnataka , brought up and studied in Coimbatore tamilnadu
Obstacles made me to overcome as writer , writing is my passion

I am an aspiring writer as storyteller, a poet. I am not a well known writer or a poet or a storyteller but i am trying all my best so that people around can read me.

An Introvert. A chaos. Ashish spills his emotions through writings. He connects himself more with Hindi and Urdu poetry and his work talks about hope, struggles and unrequited love.
He is a resident of Meerut and is presently pursuing his Post Graduation in Optometry and Vision Science in Hyderabad.

I express *my feelings in my*
poetries.

I *am a businessmen. poetry is my*
hobby.and now this hobby is giving me
an identity. I hope that one day my
hobby should take me to higher levels

ABOUT REASONS AND LAUGHTER

Reasons and Laughter is a community which deals with providing services, compiling anthologies, organising competitions and Open Mics, found by Japneet Kaur.

Our main objective is to give a good platform to budding writers to help them grow, even to provide best services and giving wings to their dreams.

Email: ralservicess@gmail.com

Instagram: @reasons_and_laughter